Walt Disney's
Winnie-the-Pooh
and the
HONEY PATCH

A GOLDEN BOOK • NEW YORK
Western Publishing Company, Inc.
Racine, Wisconsin 53404

QRST

It was a fine spring morning when Owl and Pooh decided to take a walk. Owl ruffled his feathers in the warm air.

"The atmospheric conditions . . ." he began.

"Indeed," Pooh said.

Owl went on. ". . . and the prevailing winds mean that it is now time for—"

"Honey," Pooh interrupted.

"Honey?" said Owl impatiently. "Pooh, you are a Bear of Little Brain and Too Much Tummy. I was talking about *spring!* Spring is the time of the year when everything starts growing."

"I should say it's also a good time for Someone to eat honey," Pooh replied. "Especially me."

Owl continued, speaking more loudly. "Spring is the time for Rabbit to plant carrot seeds, and for Piglet to plant small cabbage plants. Then they can eat carrots and cabbages all year long."

"All year long?" Pooh repeated. He had a lovely thought. "Owl, do you suppose that if I plant one of my honey pots, it will grow honey?"

"That sounds like a Practical Idea," Owl said. "But, then again, maybe it isn't. You see, Pooh—"

But Pooh wasn't listening. He was too busy thinking about a whole year's supply of honey in his very own honey patch.

That afternoon, Rabbit strolled past Pooh's house and heard him inside, pondering. "This big one? That small one? I shouldn't waste the big one—but a small one wouldn't grow much honey. Maybe I'll plant a middle-sized one."

"What are you planting?" Rabbit asked.

"Owl has given me a Practical Idea," Pooh explained. "I shall grow honey from a honey pot."

"That *is* a Practical Idea," Rabbit replied. "I'll help you with it."

So the two friends planted one middle-sized pot deep in the ground.

Before long, Rabbit's carrots poked through the ground, and Piglet's cabbage plants looked bigger. Pooh's honey pot, however, wasn't growing anything at all.

"Poor Pooh! I can't understand what's wrong," Rabbit told Piglet and Eeyore. "Maybe we should talk to Owl. He knows the scientifics about growing."

But when they asked Owl what was wrong, he ruffled his feathers and looked cross. "It wasn't *my* idea to grow honey from a pot! It was Pooh's idea!" he exclaimed. "Actually, I wondered from the beginning if it was a Practical Idea."

"Poor Pooh!" sighed Rabbit.

"Maybe we can *make* it work," Piglet squeaked in a Very Excited Voice. "When Pooh is sleeping, we can dig up the honey pot. Perhaps if you look at it, Owl, you'll see what is wrong."

"I don't think—" Owl began. But they all looked at him so hopefully that he stopped right there.

That night, they crept carefully to the edge of Pooh's honey patch.

Rabbit whispered, "I think a Very Small Animal should dig up a honey pot."

"Me?" Piglet squealed softly.

"Unless you're afraid," Rabbit replied.

Piglet marched bravely into the patch and began to dig. The deeper he went, the more the hole seemed like a place where a Very Large Animal might come to rest in the dark.

Thump. He struck something hard.

He pulled and tugged. Suddenly the honey pot came free, and Piglet tumbled over backward.

"Help!" cried Piglet, thinking a whole herd of Very Large Animals was upon him.

"Look! The pot's broken," Eeyore said. "Now we'll never know what was wrong."

Somehow Owl felt better.

"We must find another pot," Rabbit said firmly.

"I don't have a pot, but I do have a bucket I can spare," said Piglet.

He hurried home, with all the others for company, and they carried the bucket back to Pooh's honey patch.

"I think," said Owl, "that what *this* honey pot needs is sun and air and an occasional rain. Those are important for growing. We'll fill up the hole, and we'll put the bucket—here—on top. And we'll see what happens."

That was what they did. And that was why there was a bucket in the honey patch when Pooh hurried out the next morning. He wanted to see if anything exciting might have happened during the night.

He stared at the bucket in astonishment. *Think, think, think,* he said to himself. *My honey pot didn't grow honey, but it did grow a bucket. A very fine bucket, too. And a bucket is most useful when it is filled with something sweet.*

HONEY

Off he stumped into the woods to find something sweet to put in his bucket. He made up this hum to keep him company:

If a bear in the summer,
Clankety, clinkety,
Has a garden to sow,
Clinkety, clankety,
It's much better to sing,
Clankety, clinkety,
Than to wait for his honey to grow.

He wished Piglet were with him to sing the *clinkety's* and *clankety's.* Piglet would like that.

While Pooh was off collecting honey, Rabbit, Piglet, Eeyore, and Owl stopped by to see if the bucket had grown anything.

"It's gone!" Rabbit exclaimed. "First no honey, then no honey pot, and now no bucket."

"I knew it," said Eeyore gloomily. "I could have guessed that this would happen."

They were about to ask Owl what to do next, when
Pooh came out of the woods.

"Hurrah!" shouted Pooh, hurrying toward his friends.
"Company for breakfast!"

"Pooh!" Rabbit shouted back. "You've filled our
bucket with honey. How wonderful!"

"*Your* bucket?" Pooh asked. "Well, you are welcome
to share, of course, but I did find this bucket growing
here in *my* honey patch. And the handle makes it very
useful for honey-finding time."

The others smiled while Piglet explained exactly how the bucket happened to grow in the honey patch. And then the friends all sat down together for a breakfast of honey.

"It's delicious," Piglet said, "but honey is certainly easier to find than it is to grow, wouldn't you say, Pooh?"

"Indeed," said Pooh.

"I hope you've learned that growing honey in the garden is not a Practical Idea after all," said Owl. "Still, with my knowledge of the atmosphere and the prevailing winds . . ."

"Indeed," said Pooh again.

". . . our spring planting has yielded quite a fine crop!" Owl concluded proudly.

"Indeed," Pooh said once more, and he licked the last of the honey off his paws.